NANIMA

Spiritual Fiction

NANIMA SERIES
BOOK I

DONNA GODDARD

Second Edition 2023

Published by Donna Goddard

Victoria, Australia

Paperback ISBN: 978-0645822649

Large Print ISBN: 978-0645875539

Cover design by Donna Goddard

www.donnagoddard.com

CONTENTS

THE DANCING HUNTER

HANDS THAT HOLD

THE HELPFUL MASTER'S
MAN AND THE BACK DOCTOR

PART II
SPIRITS WITHOUT BODIES

ALTER OF SACRIFICE

EXISTENTIAL STICKING POINT

THE DREAMING

BREATH-BASED

PART I
SPIRITS WITH BODIES

DISCOVERY

CHAPTER 1

NANIMA

N anima lay in a pretty-as-a-picture valley at the joining point of two living, breathing rivers. The small country town had an English name, but Nanima was its ancient-as-the-rivers Aboriginal one.

When discovering it, English explorer Oxley said, "It is beautifully picturesque."

Of course, he didn't really discover it. Even before the local people knew it, the valley and rivers knew themselves. The idea of discovery and possession belongs to those who cannot see the value in lives other than their own.

The Aboriginal people had a different sense of ownership. There is no need to possess anything when there is access to everything. It is only when someone says that your mother belongs to them that there is a problem. For more than fifty thousand years, there wasn't a problem. For the last two hundred, there was.

Oxley also said, "The valley is studded with fine trees upon a soil which may be equalled but can never be excelled."

When you live from the land, which ultimately all of us do, soil is everything. Forgetting this is at our peril. The rich Nanima soil spread its generosity well beyond the banks of the rivers and fed the trees, the long-time people, the soon-to-arrive Chinese who would befriend the Aborigines as fellow under-rated people, and the incoming white folk with their eyes on grain and stock.

Amongst the early white settlers were men who were good and men who were bad. Either way, the soil and rivers fed them, their children, and their grandchildren.

One of those grandchildren had recently returned to Nanima after a thirty-year absence. The pull of the land, the beat of the waterways, and the voiceless voice of the neither black-nor-white earth spirit beckoned Maliyan back.

CHAPTER 2

MALIYAN

After school, Maliyan left Nanima for the city and rarely came back. Now that she had returned, she decided to use her indigenous nickname. She wasn't Aboriginal, but the name was affectionately given to her by an Aboriginal boyfriend in high school.

She wanted a fresh outlook. How we name things is closely connected with how we perceive them. Why else would colonisers rename everything? Although Maliyan didn't have Aboriginal blood in her, she considered the indigenous people part of her country's fibre. So, she considered them part of her. She was pretty sure they didn't feel the same about her.

The name Maliyan meant wedge-tailed eagle to the Wiradjuri mob. Her teenage boyfriend said that one day, she would fly away. As it turned out, it was he who flew away. He died in a drowning accident. Almost certainly, life would have separated them soon enough, but when such a course is abruptly derailed, we can become part of its buried unresolve.

After three decades of work in the city, Maliyan had

enough money to buy a small, somewhat rundown coal miner's cottage and enough to live on—if she lived simply. Simple was precisely what she intended to do.

As she walked, she pondered how everyone walks everywhere in a country town, especially the children. Although most people are unaware of it, walking automatically connects bodies to the land. All the temperature changes are keenly felt when little divides the body from its surroundings. Nanima had a relatively comfortable climate, but the local children had endless memories of crunching through frost-kissed grass or sweltering in the summer heat.

Passing the last shop before home, Maliyan gazed at her reflection in the window. Her hair was short. Her face was clear and clean. Healthy, well-balanced people have uncomplicated faces. Faces only become complicated after years of layering from mental and emotional stress. Her body was, in the words of her city chiropractor, "age-appropriate". It was meant to be a compliment of the highest order. "Don't get me started on the grossly avoidable problems most people have with their bodies through laziness and compulsions," he would say.

Chiropractors tend to have a multi-level type of intelligence. They have to be academically smart enough to get through the years of medical training. They also have to be emotionally and spiritually mature enough to understand the energetic part of their work, which is considered equally important. It makes for a coherent and intuitive type of health professional, which, unfortunately, is uncommon.

On Maliyan's recent visit to her chiropractor, he asked, "Did you get something special for Christmas?"

"Not particularly," said Maliyan with not a trace of self-pity. "I suppose you did because you have a wife."

"Not particularly," said the chiropractor with a smile. "I'm more the one to do that. She's a last-minute panic shopper."

Yes, thought Maliyan, *that's exactly what you would do—think about a lovely present and make an effort to arrange it.*

"Enjoy your new life in the country," said the chiropractor at the end of the appointment. "I envy you."

Maliyan smiled at him. People like him don't envy. Happy people don't compare themselves with others. If they like something in another person, it inspires them to do something a little different in themselves. They don't waste energy on jealousy.

"What's stopping you?" asked Maliyan.

The chiropractor pointed to his office and the pictures of his family on the desk.

"One day," he said.

Maliyan doubted that. He had too much in the city. Besides, it is one thing to pack up a single life and completely reroute it. It is quite another when it involves the lives of other people. As the African proverb says,

> *If you want to go fast, go alone.*
> *If you want to go far, go together.*

There is one place you can go as fast and as far as you want, thought Maliyan. *It's the inner journey. That one, you don't have a choice. You have to go alone.*

DUMP

CHAPTER 3

BAG OF BONES

"How's your body?" asked Gary.

Not many people ask for personal information about your body so outrightly. Your chiropractor does.

"You didn't do the five-hour drive this morning, did you?"

Nanima was far enough away from the city to be inaccessible to day-trippers. It meant that the bulk of people out there in the sticks were committed to country life.

"No, I came yesterday," said Maliyan. "Going back after here. I have a question for you."

Gary was the sort of person who loved questions. He could usually answer them and, if the client would allow, give a university-grade synopsis of the issue.

"I don't know why," said Maliyan, "but I get really nervous when I have to come here."

Her body was in a good state, and the cracking didn't hurt. There was no logical reason to feel afraid of it.

"I don't mind when you crack my spine, legs, or hips,"

13

continued Maliyan. "It's my neck. To be exact, the right side of my neck."

"I'm not a psychologist," said Gary.

He knew he was heading down the wrong track as soon as he said the words. The shadow of indignation that passed over Maliyan's face would have, anyway, told him. She was not lacking in psychological sophistication.

"I tell myself that it doesn't hurt and that there is no need to get anxious about it," said Maliyan. "I visualise myself as a bag of bones going to the mechanic for servicing."

Gary laughed. Not heartily. He was too earnest for that.

Maliyan didn't explain her more subtle pre-appointment procedure of distancing herself from her body. Her yogic interest had given her numerous processes for developing a small space between herself and her body and mind. In this way, even if we are suffering from something, it will not have such an impact on our inner stability.

"Does that help?" asked Gary, referring to her bag of bones visualisation.

"Not really," said Maliyan.

He turned his attention to cracking her body and eventually came to the culprit area.

After doing the non-offending side of her neck, he said, "You are not demonstrating any muscular tension when I crack you."

"I can relax my body when I want to," said Maliyan. "That's not the problem."

He moved to the offending side of her neck and gave it a skilful, painless crack. He had no nervousness about assaulting bodies. He said it was similar to driving at speed with oncoming traffic a mere few feet away and only a white line separating the two. He said he knew where the line was.

Something surprising then happened. Tears surfaced in Maliyan's eyes—from the jolting of the white bones through the fiery communication tracks of the body to the bottomless cavities of her eyes. Maliyan wasn't a crier. She wasn't opposed to it, but didn't usually feel the need at this stage of her life.

Clapping his hands together as if he had just won a prize, Gary said, "Ahh, that I know!"

Maliyan assumed that the "that" he was referring to was the tears.

"That I know," repeated Gary, "because many people cry when they are cracked."

Maliyan pushed on her arms to get off the cracking bed, but Gary gently placed her back down. He walked around the bed and thought. He wanted his few sentences to be precisely right.

"I'm not just cracking bags of bones," he said in teacher mode. "Every part of your body is attached to your brain and numerous energy centres. Your neck, in particular, is intricately interwoven with your brain function. When I crack your neck, it gives your brain a major dump of information. It feels like an overload, even though most people are unaware of it happening."

"Yes," said Maliyan as triumphantly as Gary. "That's it! My original presenting problem was the right side of my neck. I must store a lot of karmic refuse there. The sudden, big karmic dumping makes me nervous, not the actual bone cracking."

Gary translated what he assumed karmic dumping meant into his language and was satisfied with the result.

"See you in a month?" he asked.

Maliyan nodded. It was a very productive fifteen minutes. Productivity is far more related to undivided attention and openness than time.

❧

AS SHE BEGAN HER LONG DRIVE BACK TO NANIMA, Maliyan pondered, *It's one thing to know it's karmic dumping, but what exactly is it dumping? What precisely is in the load?*

She turned her neck—a neck which was now much more flexible—and looked through the rear window. There was a long line of Friday freeway traffic heading homeward or weekend-getaway-ward.

Who am I kidding? she thought. *It's not that we don't know what we have buried away in the bones and sinews of our bodies. We know. We were the ones who put it there, but there comes a time when we are ready to deal with the dump (or at least, smaller bits of it), and then our entire system becomes cleaner, lighter, and brighter.*

EUROKA

CHAPTER 4

BELL RIVER

Euroka lived in a hut on the Bell. It was the smaller of the two rivers that joined in Nanima. The Bell ran along the back side of the town and then into the bigger, more impressive Wambul.

"Ah," said Euroka with a grin of white teeth, "you've come down the Bell to see me on Valentine's Day."

Maliyan ignored him. Unless he had changed, Euroka was not a man looking for a valentine.

"I wasn't sure if you still lived here," said Maliyan.

"Always here," said Euroka, "except when it floods, and the backwash from the Wambul reaches my house. Otherwise, been here my whole adult life. Speaking of years, I haven't seen you for a few."

Maliyan looked, in turn, at the hut, the vegetable garden, and the river bank bordered with old gums.

"Looks the same," she said.

"Why change what don't need changin'," said Euroka.

Maliyan noted his grammar and thought, *He has always been a sage type of person, but not an educated one. He is educated by everything but the education system.*

"Learned all I know from this 'ere river," said Euroka. "Rivers know it all. Nothin' worth knowin' that they don't know."

Euroka held his eyes on his beloved river—his lifelong companion. He stood in a comfortably commanding way. His long, grey-white, curly hair was tied in a loose ponytail. His build was slim but strong from outdoor life. His face had many lines. His eyes had many powers. He was a mixture of features—Aboriginal, Chinese, and English. His broad nose was Aboriginal. His skin tone was naturally white but tanned from constant sun exposure. His expressive eyes were Chinese. He was one of the many cousins of Maliyan's teenage boyfriend, although he said he belonged to no one and everyone.

CHAPTER 5

BONE AND STONE

These days, Euroka had quite a reputation as a photographic artist, not that he cared for fame or money. He occasionally sold his works for his financial needs and gave the rest of the money to the local Aboriginal mission.

Glancing through the open door of Euroka's hut, Maliyan saw a pile of large artworks leaning against the wall. It was a small hut, and Euroka did big works. There was only space for one of them on the wall. It was an image of him lying naked in the dirt in the middle of bush-land. That was his trademark—him naked, somewhere in the Australian bush.

Another image showed him in a muddy waterway. The way it was constructed, you couldn't tell if he was trying to crawl into the water or tunnel into the land like a wombat. One of the most moving photographs was of Euroka lying in a recently burnt-out forest. He was smeared in ash and covered in sticks and twigs. Everything about it shook with grief. You could almost smell the fire's trail through the picture.

A striking quality of the images was that Euroka could take on either male or female form. He oscillated between the two. He was able to turn his still-flexible, sixty-year-old body into gender-bending shapes. He had a straight-up-and-down body rather than the broad shoulders of a strongly masculine type. His shoulders and hips almost matched in size. With no extra fat, he did not have the giveaway pot belly that many older males parade.

For the female images, he let his long hair flow. He knew how to shape his hips to carry a feminine line. More than that, he channelled feminine energy.

In all the photographs, Euroka had his back to the camera. Otherwise, his prizewinning pictures would have been classed as pornography. They had no sense of the sexual in them. Or if they did, it could only be classed as the great orgasm of creation's exploding passion or the gentle beauty of a bud shyly raising its head sunwards. It seemed the most natural thing in the world for Euroka to be unclothed because how else could one claim one's maternal heritage but by being blood and bone, dirt and stone?

In the photograph on the hut wall, Euroka was looking decidedly male. Although he had definite techniques to bring out his masculinity in the male-based photographs, one feature stood out in this picture—his hairy male backside.

CHAPTER 6

GUWAYU

Being Valentine's Day, Maliyan had been thinking about her past loves. If you are a loving person, you will have loved many people by the time you are fifty. Even if you have been married to the same person for thirty years, in your heart of hearts, you'll have loved others. Humans are like that.

"Happy Valentine's Day," said Euroka as Maliyan prepared to leave.

Remembering a quote by Kahlil Gibran, she said, "Between what is said and not meant, and what is meant and not said, most of love is lost."

"Yep," said Euroka. "Don't say what you don't mean, and do say what you do. Guwayu."

"Guwayu—see you soon," said Maliyan.

HIGH

CHAPTER 7

RIVALRY

L ike Maliyan, the woman in the chiropractic waiting room travelled a long way to Gary. She came from a vibrant, alternative town, Byron Bay, on the far north coast. As she had let out a few low screaming-type sounds when Gary had been attending to her, on returning to the reception area, she apologised to everyone that it probably sounded like a torture chamber. She was a confident, talkative woman. Seeing that Maliyan was engaged, she continued the conversation specifically with her.

"It doesn't hurt," she said, "so I don't know why I react like that."

As this was precisely the topic Maliyan and Gary had discussed a month ago, Maliyan told her a version of the karmic-dumping idea.

Being from Byron Bay, the woman understood and continued, "I get so nervous before I come."

"Don't worry about trying to make yourself less afraid," said Maliyan. "Maybe, just accept that the energetic process can be a bit unpleasant sometimes, but it's well worth it."

For a moment, the woman seemed to think that was an excellent idea, but then her expression changed to one of slight annoyance. Maliyan concluded that she probably had a yogic following or spiritual group back home and was used to being the teacher, not the taught (especially by some unknown person in the reception area). She most likely also considered herself Gary's favourite client and confidante in all things spiritual.

Gary is like one of those mothers, thought Maliyan, *who gives the impression to all her children that they are secretly the favourite.*

CHAPTER 8

CBA

"I t's the CBA," said Gary.

"Commonwealth Bank of Australia?" asked Maliyan.

She said that because her father had worked for the C.B.A. many years ago.

Looking at her oddly, Gary said, "No, cost-benefit analysis."

They had been talking about the use of anti-inflammatories for injuries.

"You have to weigh up whether the cost is worth the benefit," said Gary. "The other day, one of my sons asked for my opinion about a particular girl he was interested in. Generally, I try not to interfere with my kids' lives."

"I'm sure you don't," said Maliyan.

"I told him that CBA is a technique for comparing the positive and negative impact of using certain resources," said Gary. "Firstly, you have to specify the options. In his case, go out with the girl or not. Secondly, you have to decide which costs and benefits will count. In his case, I assume the ones that count are sex, company, and social status. Thirdly, you have to identify measurement indicators for the decision's impact. In his case, a scale of happiness to heartbreak. Fourthly, you must consider the decision's impact over its lifetime."

"So," asked Maliyan, "how did that all go?"

"Eventually, to make it simple for him," said Gary, "I told him, 'Look, buddy, the positives are that she's hot, exciting, and other guys want her. The negatives are that she's, excuse the language, a fucking head-case.'"

Maliyan laughed and said, "What did he decide?"

Gary smiled and said, "I think he was punching above his weight, and the decision might have been taken out of his hands."

CHAPTER 9

CBD

One hour into her drive home, Maliyan stopped in the small town at the highest point of her ascent up the mountain range. The skyline of the CBD (Central Business District) was visible in the distance. She breathed in the fresh air. Not as clean as Nanima, but way cleaner than what was below her in the city sprawl.

As she strolled along, she noticed a sign on a shop noticeboard.

Get high with us at High.
Join us for Elemental Essentials.
Starts today!

Although she still had a four-hour drive home, she decided to attend the event.

Right now, I am without partner, dependents, pets, and work, thought Maliyan, *so if not now, when? When to spontaneously do such things?*

With that, she set off on the twenty-minute drive into the mountainous bushland, in pursuit of getting high.

CHAPTER 10

ELEMENTAL ESSENTIALS

The community was easy to spot with its large, metal *High* sign overlooking the majestic slopes to the city. The name was a reference to the physical location and the spiritual path being a natural inner high.

It was a happy coincidence that the entrance to High had a wooden statue of a wedge-tailed eagle (Maliyan's namesake). It was carved from the remains of a dead eucalyptus tree about sixteen feet tall.

Beneath it was a bowl of mud mixture with instructions:

The mud connects us with the first essential element—earth. Please apply the mud to the following points on your body:

1. between your eyebrows
2. the pit of your throat
3. the point where your rib cage meets
4. your naval
5. your palms
6. the soles of your feet

Although the community was of the yogic-Hindu tradition, their outreach was nondenominational, and their requirements for participation in all processes were inclusive.

What could be more yogic than mud and chakras, thought Maliyan as she pasted herself with the mixture while sitting cross-legged on the grass with about fifty other participants.

She then remembered that Ash Wednesday in the Catholic Church was two days ago. It marks the start of Lent, the forty days leading up to Easter. Easter itself is set by the cycles of the moon, shifting each year.

On Ash Wednesday, the priest puts ash on your forehead and says, "Remember that you are dust, and to dust, you shall return."

How yogic, thought Maliyan. *Earth, dust, ash, and mud are not just yogic or Catholic ideas, but universal ones. Religions are far more similar than they are different.*

"Welcome to our community," said a woman, around forty, in white clothing. "Patanjali, the father of modern yoga, begins the *Yoga Sutras* with these words, 'And now yoga.' We are ready when we have tried everything else and know it doesn't work. We are ready for yoga. We are ready for the spiritual path. Let us chant together, *Yoga Yoga Yogeshwaraya*. Yoga means union, and Yogeshwaraya is to transcend the physical domain."

After a few rounds, Maliyan picked up the chant, and something about its rhythmic, lulling, stabilising, intense yet calming nature brought a sense of union.

Yoga Yoga Yogeshwaraya
Bhuta Bhuta Bhuteshwaraya
Kala Kala Kaleshwaraya
Shiva Shiva Sarveshwaraya
Shambho Shambho Mahadevaya

CATHEDRAL

CHAPTER 11

THIEF OR SAINT

I t was almost dark as Maliyan entered the large country town at the bottom of the mountain descent on her way home from High. She still had three more hours' drive, but seeing the lights shining through the magnificent stained-glass windows of the cathedral, she decided to stop. This town had a lot of money at one stage, and the cathedral was built as a grand rural monument. It was truly majestic, commanding its own small hill facing the mountain cliffs.

Mass was finished, but the woman at the door said it would be fine for Maliyan to sit somewhere while they packed up. Maliyan headed straight for the back row, as far away from the straggling congregation as possible. Her footsteps echoed on the long walk to the end of the cathedral. These days, churches are generally closed except for services, so she was glad to have the opportunity to be inside.

There's something wrong with that, thought Maliyan. *These powerful places of accumulated prayer have healing energy in the air, and here they are, all locked up with no one being able to benefit.*

Although she understood the security issues, she felt sure that the churches themselves must be sad not to use the many years of prayer, heartbreak, laughter, love, and every other human emotion shared with the Divine.

There must be another solution, she thought. *If people could see the energy, they would not lock the buildings up. But they cannot see it, and even if they could, they wouldn't know what to do with it.*

Whenever she had a chance, Maliyan went into empty churches of any denomination. If someone was about, they generally looked at her like she must be quite saintly. It made Maliyan smile.

In reality, she thought, *I am sneaking in, like a thief, to steal some energy. It's a matter of perspective.*

CHAPTER 12

CHARITY

A s soon as Maliyan sat down and looked high above her at the magnificent wood ceiling and far in front of her at the pristine marble altar, tears came to her eyes. They were tears brought on by the majesty and pure beauty of it all. She put her hands over her face so no one could see her. That way, she was free to have the moment be used in whatever healing way the energy wished rather than worrying about other people's reactions to her.

Predictably, when Maliyan was leaving, the woman at the door, who had probably been watching her, politely tried to engage her in a conversation. The woman, no doubt, assumed that something was upsetting Maliyan. I guess that's what happens when you cover your face with your hands and sit on your own, far away from everyone else.

The woman was one of those lovely senior ladies who —having raised her children, been blessed with grandchildren, and graced with a long, positive marriage—dedicates most of her free time to charity work. Such women feel grateful that they have gotten thus far without some catastrophe, such as a child dying, a traumatic marriage breakup, the loss of a loved family home, or a debilitating illness. Or, if they have had to endure one or more of these sorrows, they are the sort of person to pick themselves up and make something out of the mess, so much so that other people down the track wouldn't know about their past dramas.

They always have a gracious, ready smile, wear sensible shoes, and have a cardigan and umbrella on hand if the weather turns bad. Bless them. Where would our communities be without them? They hold the fibre of families, churches, and every imaginable community project together. The only thing was that Maliyan didn't need her charity.

"With all that's wrong in the world," said the woman tentatively, "it can feel like we have the weight of it on our shoulders."

She said it as a question and gave Maliyan the chance to express her sorrow at whatever was supposedly causing her grief. For a moment, Maliyan thought about making something up as she didn't want the woman to feel that she had failed in her responsibilities, but that would have been ridiculous. Somehow, it didn't seem appropriate to say, *I was overcome with the beauty of the place.* It would have sounded a little pretentious. She decided not to answer her directly and, instead, pointed around at the cathedral.

"It's so..." she started.

However, before she got any more words out, the tears returned. Deciding that this would only further confuse the kind woman, she stopped talking. After that, the woman's expression changed from motherly duty to interest and curiosity.

CHAPTER 13

MASTERS

"Where do you come from, dear?" asked the woman.

"Nanima," answered Maliyan.

"Oh, really?" said the woman. "My nephew and his family have just moved to Nanima. He is in charge of a two-year project in Thubbo. However, the housing shortage there means they have ended up renting in Nanima, which is much prettier anyway. My nephew and his wife, Kat, have a ten-year-old boy. They would be in their late forties now. They didn't have him until later because Kat had a successful career as a dancer and wanted to retire before child-raising. She said that it wasn't essential to do so and that other dancing mums don't, but, for her, parenting came first—by a long shot."

"What sort of dancing?" asked Maliyan, who, for some reason, felt something ignite in her.

"Ballroom dancing," said the woman. "Kat was a latin dancer. Now that the boy is older, she will start a ballroom dancing school in Nanima, at least for the duration of their stay."

"Is it just for children?" asked Maliyan, who was becoming far more excited about the dance school than she would have expected.

"No," said the woman. "Ballroom dancing is one of those wonderful dance forms that has an active place for all age groups. I have friends who do competitive ballroom dancing, and they are in their seventies. Masters 4, I think they call it."

"Does being in Masters make you a master," asked Maliyan, "or does it just mean you are old?"

Pointing to a flashing sign next door, which read *Cathedral Motel*, the woman said, "It's getting late, dear. The motel sits under the wing of this cathedral. You couldn't get a safer place to rest your head for the night."

☙❧

MALIYAN STOOD UNDER THE MOTEL SHOWER FOR A LONG time. The little bathroom was clean, and the shower had a strong flow of hot water.

How healing water is, thought Maliyan. *That's because it is one of the main elements of life. We are more than 70% water, so we respond to it readily. It doesn't just clean our bodies. That's the least of it. It cleans our etheric body. That's why almost everyone feels better after a long shower.*

Although Maliyan understood the problem of long-haired women who didn't want to dry their mass of hair every night, she felt that they didn't understand what they were missing out on by not having a daily stream of water directly on the crown of their heads, which is the primary energy intake location of the body.

Hair fashion or health? thought Maliyan. *That's not even a choice.*

TRUTH BE TOLD

CHAPTER 14

AUTUMNAL BITE

The water in the rock pool of the Bell was warm compared to the coolness of the running flow a few feet away. Maliyan lay back in the quiet, inviting space. She saw her dress on the branch, moving slightly in the breeze. The sky was bright and blue. A few cloud-puffs jollied themselves by playing with the sun. Although this morning had a typical autumnal cold bite, this afternoon's sun had a typical autumnal hot bite. The heat was subdued by the branches of the gum trees along the river. All in all, it was entirely pleasant.

Maliyan took a deep breath and sank to the bottom of the rock pool. She kept her eyes open. After rain, the river water was usually brown with mud, but today it was transparent. She watched the sunlight bounce off the water's surface above. The bottom of the Bell gave a different perspective on things. That's why she came. She intended to visit Euroka, but his hut was locked, which meant he was away on an extended trip. Deciding that the Bell was a better sage than Euroka anyway, she wandered along its banks until she arrived at the rock pool.

The adult dance class started last week in Nanima. Disappointingly, on the first day, Maliyan got a sudden back pain severe enough to prevent her from going. The same thing happened today, and she missed the second class. As the saying goes,

Fool me once; shame on you.
Fool me twice; shame on me.

Deciding that the only fool in the situation was herself, she set to work on uncovering the back pain's message.

Truth be told (and the Bell was a place for truth to be told), ballroom dancing was not a new venture for Maliyan. She had been involved with it for ten years. When she was thirty, she started having lessons. Over time, she was given several opportunities to partner with people. Her favourite partner was during the last few years of her dancing. As often happens with favourites, it had a less-than-favourite ending.

You would think the connection between a new and old dance situation would be obvious, but we are masters at not seeing the obvious. So, our body takes on the connection for us. Once we relieve it of this responsibility, it usually jumps for joy and jumps right out of whatever physical predicament it had to acquire on our behalf.

CHAPTER 15

BODY TALK

After rising for a few breaths, Maliyan sank back into the silent depths of the Bell. She recalled that when she first started dancing, it was an instant love affair—with dance. Dance ignited something in her that was different to everything else inside her. A long-lost part of herself was breathing again. She wasn't sure how long it had been lost, but was glad to have it re-found. The fact that it was also good for her health was an auxiliary to her pure pleasure in moving her body. Add another person, and it multiplies the joy, at least at various points along the way.

Her last partner, Rex, was a good male dancer—better than her, which is worth a lot. After a while, he fell in love with her. After more of a while, she fell in love with him. They fell in love in somewhat different ways. He fell in love in the usual way. She fell in love in a conscious way. One of the reasons she did so was because he was married. That is always problematic. However, it's not overly problematic if you fall in love consciously because what you want is different.

49

This land of her heritage had given Maliyan a gift. It came with birth but only showed itself as she matured. Men tended to fall in love with her. Not all men, only some, but more than you would expect. She was not particularly fall-in-love-with sort of material. She was only ordinarily attractive—attractive in the way everyone is when they are healthy and happy. Her only sexiness was in her connection to the earth. All other sexiness didn't even make sense to her. She wasn't particularly focused on men, as she tended not to see people as men or women.

Over the years, Maliyan figured out that her love triggered the falling-in-love reaction. That was the entirety of it. It seems simple enough, but if you tell people who want more of that sort of thing to love more, they generally say (and are quite convinced) that they are already very loving. That's because they do not understand the difference between love and need. Need is often dressed as love, but it is always self-concerned. Love can be dressed any old way it wants, but it will always be concerned with the good of the other.

Whoever receives such a gift can never use it for their own purposes. That is the unwritten but unalterable rule. If the rule is broken, the gift is removed. Worse than that, one would get very bad karma for abusing it. Luckily, the gift itself—the gift of love—ensures that it is unlikely to be abused, but it is possible.

Regardless of what Maliyan understood about love, it did not mean that those who fell in love with her understood anything at all. And therein lay another problem. When normal people fall in love, they want a lot of unstated stuff—ridiculous stuff. If they don't get it, they tend to get angry and do a lot of ridiculous stuff. That's when endings happen. For Maliyan, endings didn't happen.

Situations can certainly end, but love doesn't end. Otherwise, it isn't love, is it?

Perhaps it would be wiser not to let people fall in love with you. One could organise that. It wouldn't be hard. Just change the energy you give out, which would change the response. However, as problematic as falling in love is, it serves a valuable purpose. When someone falls in love with you, they become open in a way they are generally not. That means you can influence them. Yes, it's a risk. You have to accept the danger of them turning into a psychopath. But there is also the possibility of them learning something valuable that may otherwise take lifetimes. It's worth the risk.

Shaking the water off, Maliyan pulled her sun-warmed dress over her shoulders. She moved her back and had no pain. She didn't know whether her backache was gone for good or would return. She wasn't sure how much work needed to go into this memory. The karmic dumping ground of our body is the storehouse of many memories. Her body would soon enough let her know. Bodies have their own highly effective way of doing the talking.

THE DANCING HUNTER

CHAPTER 16

MOUTHS THAT OPEN DOORS

At one stage, Nanima had a thriving business centre. Nowadays, half the shops were empty. Broken windows and dusty, cobwebby exteriors were the unfortunate norm. The larger country towns, such as Thubbo, were expanding, and the smaller ones were declining. The bigger towns had a monopoly on businesses, jobs, housing, and services. It was a self-perpetuating cycle. Nanima's old dance school was one of the casualties. Its peeling pink paint was a tell-tale sign. Kat was able to rent it for a song or, in her case, a dance.

As Maliyan walked towards the dance school entrance, a black Land Rover pulled up at speed. A dark-haired man hurriedly jumped out. He was probably about fifty but much more sprightly than the average, middle-aged country fella. He opened the back door and grabbed his dance shoes as she passed the car. They were lying on top of several guns. Maliyan thought that he looked too citified to be a farmer. His four-wheel drive was too clean. She assumed he was a recreational hunter.

"On my way to a hunting trip after here," said the man

by way of explanation. "That's why I could say yes when Kat asked me to come. I'm always busy in the city, but my trips out here keep me going. I'm happiest when covered in dirt and blood."

After seeing the look on Maliyan's face, which was generally very readable, the dancing hunter smiled broadly to counteract the image he was possibly portraying. He was a good-looking man, and his large, enthusiastic smile made him more so. In some ways, it embodied the quintessential Australian spirit. Yet, it wasn't quite the grin of the country lad, which was simple, cheerful, and mischievous.

He was a little too intense for a man born of country soil. His smile was slightly orchestrated, not insincere, but deliberate. It was the smile of an intelligent person who realised that, for a tiny movement of the body, a big smile worked disproportionate wonders in making one's way into people's hearts.

Your mouth can open many doors, thought Maliyan, *but not all.*

CHAPTER 17

GUNS AND GOATS

T he dancing hunter shuffled his guns into a safer spot, locked his car, and headed for the studio door. Having relatives who went wild-pig shooting, Maliyan was familiar with guns. Also, most farmers had them. They used them for pest control (particularly in plagues) on various animals, including rabbits, foxes, flying foxes, birds, feral cats, and even kangaroos. Although the killing process was known to her, she was not at ease with it, even less so with recreational shooting.

As soon as she was an adult, moved to the city, and had exposure to vegetarianism, she became one. As a child, she didn't know any vegetarians and had the vague idea that it was a cultural thing—maybe for people who lived in India. Once she thought about what must happen at the abattoirs, eating meat was no longer an option for her. It wasn't a matter of deciding whether she would be a meat-eater or not. The concept of a creature having to die to feed her was unpalatable when there were very good alternatives.

However, the gun issue was not as simple as deciding

whether to be a carnivore or herbivore, killing for sport or not. About five years ago, further out west, a large region of country was designated for total indigenous ranger care. They immediately caught and killed all the feral goats. There were a lot of them. The Aboriginal rangers left a small tribe of fourteen goats. The purpose of the tribe was not to keep the feral goat population going but to entice stray goats to the area so they could also be killed. They never let the tribe grow larger than fourteen.

Maliyan remembered reading about it at the time. It seemed a bit brutal, but she had to trust that the indigenous caretakers knew what they were doing. It was in their blood from tens of thousands of years of looking after the land. She recently saw a photo of that same land. On one side of the image was the white-ranger land. It was sparsely vegetated, destroyed by goats. On the other side was the black-ranger, goat-free land. It was full of vegetation and would have been home to unseen native wildlife supported by it.

Turning her mind away from guns and goats, Maliyan followed the dancing hunter through the pink doors of the old-new dance school and, for the first time in ten years, donned her dancing heels.

HANDS THAT HOLD

CHAPTER 18

LEADING ASTRAY

The dancing hunter was back. Maliyan assumed he was returning to the city from his hunting trip out west. He was a good dancer—too good for the class. She didn't know why he was even there.

There are many more women than men who want to dance, thought Maliyan. *For some reason, he is obliging Kat by partnering us.*

Partner, he certainly could. Other men were in the class, but they were the normal hotchpotch of male dancers who attend such things. The older they get, the worse they become. Despite their lack of dancing skills and physical prowess, they often think they have acquired the right to be the teacher. You can go into almost any studio and hear underperforming, middle-aged men "instructing" their female dance partners with great and utterly annoying authority, even though they usually have no idea what they are talking about.

It is what it is, thought Maliyan as she danced through the hotchpotch towards the dancing hunter.

Not only did he lead her beautifully, but he also led

everyone beautifully. His experience and sensitivity allowed him to adjust his lead from the beginners to the more experienced dancers and even to Kat. He made the clumsy women more graceful, the flighty ones more grounded, the aggressive ones more feminine, and the insecure ones more confident. He gave Kat the rare opportunity to spread her dancing wings.

Although the dancing hunter lifted Maliyan's dancing by understanding what she could and couldn't do, that was not the only thing she noticed about his partnering skills.

I don't mind him touching me, thought Maliyan.

More, she caught herself reaching out to touch him. She wondered if the other women had the same response. After looking closely, she could see that they did. Women only do that when they feel no need to protect themselves. It is a sense of trust that if they let their guard down, they will not be led astray.

She remembered one of the talks she listened to when visiting High Community in the mountains. It was about the lower chakras, sexuality, and touch. The speaker said that the binding nature of touch was why people should be very careful about who they have sex with. He said it was an energetic issue, not a moral one. He further explained that the powerful transfer of energy did not only happen through sexual interaction but could be as deep and binding (if not more) through simple, less invasive physical interactions such as holding hands.

At the time, Maliyan thought how true it was. She remembered her last dance partner. They didn't have a sexual relationship. However, the mere act of holding hands (and dancing is all about hand-holding) at frequent, regular intervals over several years was as binding as sex. It isn't necessarily that. Otherwise, every dance teacher would have a headful of intimate partners! Dance teachers, understandably, get very effective at keeping people out of their personal space.

The act of continued physical proximity combined with emotional connection is highly binding. If both links are present, the bond between two people will be cemented in their consciousness and the very structure of their bodies. They are holding each other's spirit as well as each other's body. If the relationship ends, the partners will suffer and grieve as much as they would the loss of a lover. That is how powerful touch is when it is combined with emotion. No trifling plaything!

CHAPTER 19

SENSITIVE KILLER

"How did you enjoy the class?" said a voice in the cafe.

Looking up from her coffee, Maliyan saw the dancing hunter.

"Hi," she said with surprise. "It's hard to start dancing again after so long, but I'm doing my best."

"You are doing great," he said with practised ease.

Maliyan didn't want to start blabbing on about how good he was. She was sure that if she did so, he would be off instantly. As it was, he was barely there. Like an animal in the wild that has taken the risk to stop momentarily but is ready to swing into escape mode at the slightest sniff of danger.

Deciding it was best to change the topic, she said, "How was your trip?"

"Oh, I love it out there," he said.

That must have been the right question, thought Maliyan, *because he is pulling up a chair.*

After he spoke for a while about the joys of being out bush, Maliyan said, "My cousin goes pig hunting, but he always takes his pig dogs. They are sweet at home but vicious out there."

She pointed past the gentle Nanima hills to the dry western plains and asked, "You don't take dogs?"

The dancing hunter looked slightly flustered and stood up to leave. He took a quick look at Maliyan's face and focused on her eyes. He thought that something about them reminded him of the vast expanse of outback—intimately inviting but ultimately unknowable.

He leaned closer to her and said, "My guns never left the back seat of my car."

His strongly masculine composure softened.

"Don't get me wrong. I'm a good marksman," he continued. "But I just like being out there—doing nothing. It's the only place I feel...at ease. I know it's stupid in this day and age to think that men can't be like that. I guess when it all boils down, I don't want my dad to know that I'm not that tough. Bloody hell, I can hardly say I'm going out west to be at one with nature."

Maliyan wondered if he had only told her this because there was a high possibility that he would never see her again, and he wanted to tell at least one person in his life.

While standing, he quickly drank the rest of his coffee, smiled in a way that seemed to be trying to recover his lost reputation, and waved goodbye.

Although the dancing hunter did not look at all happy with himself, Maliyan's estimation of him went up significantly. He was not the strange combination of a highly sensitive dancer and a thoughtless murderer. He was a man who had enough soul to try and find himself in God's own land. And he was a man who, at fifty, was still trying to come to terms with his own father.

THE HELPFUL MASTER'S MAN AND THE BACK DOCTOR

CHAPTER 20

FIVE HUNDRED KILOMETRES

Maliyan had not been to the city since the beginning of autumn. Perhaps it was March's march towards winter and the following months' escalating cold. That certainly made the road less inviting. Perhaps it was that she was more settled in her small-town home of, by now, six months.

This morning, however, she was not gazing at the enchanting, end-of-autumn sunrise from her garden. She was winding through the country bends, playing hide and seek with the pinks and golds of dawn.

She had two appointments in the city. The first one was for the dancing hunter's class. The second one was for the back doctor. As Maliyan's back was still complaining, Kat suggested the back doctor and, seeing as Maliyan would be in the city, passed on the information about the dancing hunter's class.

AT THE CITY DANCE STUDIO:

"Rumba," commanded the dancing hunter. "Two, three, four.... one. Two and three and four and one. Two and three and... four, one."

Dancers play with numbers because numbers are symbols for body movement. The dancing hunter had his crew in ship-shape order. They might be out of line in terms of their dancing, but no one was out of line in terms of their behaviour.

The only person who seemed to be given a little leeway was one of the annoying master's dancers. Maliyan didn't understand why. He was bordering on obnoxious. Used to being in command in his professional sphere, he brought his confident, *helpful* energy into dancing. The problem was that he shouldn't have. He didn't know what he was doing.

At one point, Maliyan was partnered with the helpful master's man. After correcting her numerous times, he ran his hand slowly along her arm. She wanted to remove it, but it would've seemed rude as the man clearly thought he was being... helpful.

The hand-down-the-arm move was something that teachers sometimes did. The dancing hunter did it himself on occasion. In his case, it was not an unwelcome intrusion. There was indeed an element of seduction in it, but it was seductive in eliciting attention and effort on the part of the recipient. It was a way of saying, *Pay attention, woman. Listen to what my body is telling you. Don't you want to dance with me? You would dance so much better if you let me dance you properly. Wouldn't you like that?* His own body would hum hypnotically with the rhythm. Seductive? You bet!

The dancing hunter happened to pass behind the helpful master's man as he was doing his hand-down-the-arm move. He rolled his eyes as if to say, *Don't listen to him. He has no idea.*

At the end of the class, the helpful master's man approached Maliyan, pointed to the dancing hunter, and said, "He neither needs nor wants a partner, but I do. Why don't you think about dancing with me?"

Maliyan had to stop herself from laughing or groaning. Seeing the master's man point to him, the dancing hunter called out, "She lives five hundred kilometres away."

The Proclaimer's old song about walking 500 miles to be with his love interest sang itself into Maliyan's mind.

She thought, *I wouldn't be the man to walk 500 miles to fall down at anyone's door, but clearly, I'm the woman willing to drive 500 kilometres to have a dance with the dancing hunter.*

The dancing hunter put his hand on the man's shoulder and said, "Don't worry, mate, I'll find you a woman."

I might drive 500 kilometres for the dancing hunter, thought Maliyan, *but I wouldn't even drive five for the helpful master's man.*

Looking like he thought the matter was far from resolved, the helpful master's man shrugged and went to get changed out of his black shirt and trousers into his work clothes.

CHAPTER 21

OUT FOR THE COUNT

"I see a lot of dancers," said the back doctor by way of explanation.

He was not only the back doctor but, to Maliyan's amazement, he was also the helpful master's man. Suddenly, everything fell into place—how Kat knew him and why the dancing hunter gave him so much, seemingly unwarranted, support.

"If it weren't for me, he wouldn't even be dancing," said the back doctor, referring to the dancing hunter. "I fixed him up and keep him going."

Maliyan did not doubt the truth of that because, for all his annoyingness on the dance floor, here in the medical room, he was brilliant. High energy, intelligent, positive, and generous. Everything you would want from a medical professional. It humbled Maliyan to think that she had written him off so quickly, and here she was absolutely needing and wanting his help.

We should take every moment, every day, and every person as new and fresh whenever we are presented with them, thought Maliyan. *That way, we won't misjudge anyone or anything. We won't miss opportunities. And nor will we carry the burden of accumulated judgements from the past.*

At the end of the appointment, Maliyan couldn't help feeling that she owed the back doctor. Was she obligated to the helpful master's man because she was obligated to the actually-helpful back doctor? She didn't know. She needn't have worried, not about that anyway.

"Sorry," said the back doctor. "You are out for the count of winter. No dancing for you until your back is better."

CHAPTER 22

LUNA TIKS

"**N**o twinkle toes with you today?" asked Luna.

Luna owned the cafe near the Nanima dance school. It was called Luna Tiks. A fortyish-year-old man, he had decided, like Maliyan, on a tree change. He moved to Nanima a few years ago. Also, like Maliyan, he had neither partner nor dependents to hinder his life change. Actually, he did have a dependent. A very well-behaved German shepherd called Iggy, whose usual place of abode was at the back door with one paw resting on the invisible line that delineated the point of no return into the cafe.

Maliyan looked at Luna and thought he was rather a twinkle toes himself.

"No," she said. "He lives in the city. He was just on his way through when you saw him."

Luna nodded. He made no effort to move away, so Maliyan kept on talking. When Luna was on, it was all systems go. Catch him on a not-infrequent bad day, and your conversation could be met with empty silence.

"I visited him a few days ago," said Maliyan.

"Long way to go for a dance," said Luna.

Luna was many things; sometimes, conflicting things. In amongst it all was kindness. He probably thought that ballroom dancing was razzle-dazzle, self-indulgent carry-on.

Nevertheless, he said, "Do what you want, my love. I do."

"I won't be doing it again any time soon," said Maliyan sadly. "The back doctor said no dancing for me all winter."

Luna hugged her and said with a wink, "You will spring back."

PART II
SPIRITS
WITHOUT BODIES

ALTER OF SACRIFICE

CHAPTER 23

DIBBIL-DIBBIL

"This is scary," whispered Luna.

Maliyan laughed but had to agree.

"What if dibbil-dibbil comes out of the cave?" said Luna.

Dibbil-dibbil was an Aboriginal word for an evil spirit. The indigenous people were never cave dwellers (probably because of dibbil-dibbil), but they did use them for male initiation ceremonies (also probably because of dibbil-dibbil).

"We'll run," said Maliyan.

Luna rolled his eyes. At least, Maliyan assumed that's what he was doing, but it was too dark to tell.

"I think this is a bad idea," said Luna. "I'm hardly a stickler for rules, but we are not allowed at the Caves when they're closed. If the white security doesn't get us, the black ghosts will."

"You worry about the spirits with bodies," said Maliyan, "and I'll take care of the ones without."

It felt like the sort of thing children do, tripping in the dark and giggling out of nerves and fun.

"Can you please point the torch ahead of us so I can find the spot?" asked Maliyan.

Luna mumbled to himself but did as he was asked.

"Luna!" scolded Maliyan. "Shine the light in front of me. I almost fell into one of the cave holes."

"Use your own fucking torch," retorted Luna. "The light doesn't just shine out of my arse, you know. You do have one, too."

"Oh, right," replied Maliyan as she turned on her own phone torch.

CHAPTER 24

WANDAANG

Yesterday evening, at Nanima Caves:
Maliyan had arrived considerably too early for the night tour yesterday evening, as she had misread the time. That was how she came to meet Wandaang. As no one was around when she got there, she climbed the hill and waited patiently next to the cave entrance.

After a while, she lay back under an old gum tree. It seemed to respond to her presence by waiving one of its branches. She looked past the branch into the night sky show, more fascinating and elaborate than any cave tour could ever be.

Seeing a figure out of the corner of her eye, Maliyan assumed it was the cave guide. When she looked at it, it disappeared, and she realised it was not a living person but a deceased one. Not a spirit with a body, but a spirit without a body. In that isolated, dark environment, she was strangely not afraid.

"I am Wandaang," said the spirit in the way spirits talk. They don't use words. They talk telepathically.

Turning towards a noise down the hill, Maliyan saw the tour guide approaching, and Wandaang disappeared.

Inside the cave:

The Bible used in the last Mass was ceremoniously left on the altar sixty years ago. Gradually, it crystallised. As it was not visible from the cave floor and no one was allowed to climb the crystal structure, it had become a thing of folklore.

The guide told Maliyan that the bible was indeed real. He recently had to climb the structure to clean off some of the green residue that forms on the crystals from visitors breathing in the space. He saw the Bible and had photo evidence.

The main Nanima cave held a large limestone and crystal formation, rising into an outcrop that resembled an altar. For decades, local Catholic priests had used it as such, until the gradual wear on the formation led, quite sensibly, to the caves being closed to all but guided tours.

The Bible used in the final Mass was left there, carefully placed on the altar, sixty years ago. Over time, it crystallised.

It could not be seen from the cave floor, and no one was permitted to climb the structure. As the years passed, it slipped into the kind of story people repeat, a tale that hovers between fact and imagination.

The guide told Maliyan it was real.

He said that not long ago, he had been required to climb the formation to clean the green film that gathers from human breath. While he was there, he saw it. The Bible, hardened into crystal.

Something once alive with human ritual and meaning was now set and preserved in a different form. It radiated silently and secretly what had crystallised within it, from deep below the earth's surface.

CHAPTER 25

SKELETONS,
SKINS, AND SKULLS

Back to this evening:

When they found the spot next to the main cave, Maliyan made Luna sit about thirty metres away because she was fairly sure that the spirit would only appear if she were alone. She was a little afraid to come alone at night—not because of the disembodied spirits but because of the bodied ones. That's why Luna was there.

Thirty metres would have to be *alone* enough for Wandaang.

"WHAT DOES HE WANT?" ASKED LUNA AS THEY HEADED back down the hill towards the car.

"He wants his bones back," said Maliyan.

"Isn't it a bit too late for that?" joked Luna.

"Not *his* bones, silly. His ancestor's bones."

"Did he say they are in the cave?"

"He said they were taken from the cave a hundred years ago and sold for museum and private collection specimens. He said that the ancestors won't rest until they are back in Country and that the land will also suffer."

"One of my customers is always bangin' on about the Repatriation Program," said Luna. "She says it's the quest to bring all the bones back to their rightful resting places so their spirits stop wandering. I guess most people want to be buried on the land they come from. It's probably instinct."

"Yes," said Maliyan, "It's instinctive because it has energetic importance. Aboriginal people got their spiritual bearings by knowing their ancestors were in certain places. It was like an energetic navigational system. I'm sure, for many, it still is. And white people would do the same if they were sufficiently connected to the land and their bodies. Anyone aware that 'from soil they come and to soil they will return' remains deeply connected to their roots."

After a pause, she continued solemnly, "It is on record that one bygone collector made a (granted) request that an Aboriginal child be shot to complete his private exhibit of skeletons, skins and skulls."

"That's horrific," said Luna.

"I remember the old Aboriginal worker on my uncle's farm," said Maliyan, "telling me about white men driving around with Aboriginal bones and skulls on their cars' dashboards. And one farmer had a swimming pool decorated with them."

Finding the conversation too sad and painful and feeling that he couldn't do anything, Luna grabbed Maliyan's hand, started running, and said, "Race you to the car."

Not much of a race if you are holding my hand, thought Maliyan, who was happier than she would have expected to have her hand be held—race or not.

EXISTENTIAL
STICKING POINT

CHAPTER 26

POISONOUS PATH

The winter solstice was turning into a cheery, bright day. Cold? Yes. Miserable? Not at all. Maliyan was enjoying the passing paddocks, stock, sky, and clouds as she drove to the nearest large country town, Thubbo. After doing her jobs, she decided to make use of the Chinese Massage Centre because Nanima didn't have one. Of all the wonderful things the Chinese bring to Australia, their massage centres were top of Maliyan's list—cheap, quick, and effective.

There was a steady stream of new staff at the Centre. Maliyan assumed they were friends and relatives of the owners on working holidays. Invariably, their English consisted of *hello, how long, pressure okay?* She didn't care about their English. If they apologised for it, she would say, "No need. You have a second language. I don't." Not that they understood what she was saying.

She did care about how proficient they were. She could tell as soon as they put their hands on her shoulders. It was a two-second transfer of information. Occasionally, she did a little experiment to see if she could guess by sight what they would be like. She couldn't. The best ones were a mixture of care, knowledge, intuition, and that healing quality some practitioners have in their hands.

Her response today was the one reserved for the best of the best. She relaxed, closed her eyes, and trustingly handed her body to the masseur. He ran his hand down her spine straight to the problematic spot.

"Poison," he said.

At least, that's what Maliyan thought he said. It was hard to tell, and there was no point trying to discuss it with him.

When Maliyan stood up, she felt quite sick instead of fantastic. On the forty-minute drive back to Nanima, it did indeed seem that low-grade poison had been released into her body. Where else could it go? It had to find a path out of her system. That's when the dreams started.

CHAPTER 27

REX THE EX

Although Maliyan was out for the count of dancing all winter, she was dancing in her dreams. She had been having recurring dreams of an argument with Rex during their dancing partnership.

The cause of the argument was minor, but the outcome was major. It had existential consequences as well as emotional ones. Existentially significant events hold powerful long-term energy and become sticking points until they are understood and rectified.

It was the first really stupid thing that Rex did. It was also the best thing he ever did.

He had been on year-long good behaviour, which showed that the relationship was important enough to him to try and make a good impression. Then, Maliyan pulled him up on something he did that hurt her. Based on his usual behaviour, she assumed he would apologise, and the matter would be fixed and forgotten.

To her surprise, his response did not diminish the ignorance or arrogance of his actions. It exacerbated them. He went on and on about why everything he did was so correct and justified. It was completely irrational. He also became insulting and offensive.

Maliyan was so shocked and saddened by his response that she ended the conversation with a one-word reply and was ready to end the relationship.

Happily, by the next day, Rex had reconsidered his position. He was apologetic, humble, and affectionate, and expressed his sincere gratitude for her—all a winning approach. If he had continued on this path, the following years would have been a different story, but the winning attitude was few and far between, becoming fewer and farther as time progressed.

Maliyan opened her eyes and saw the grey hint of sunrise before the sun got a proper foothold. She thought about the instinctiveness of the healing process, which knows precisely which event to return to in order to heal effectively. It knows which situations hold the most karma.

Go back to that first argument and that first response, Maliyan said to Rex through the eons of space and time. *That's where you went wrong. That's where you went right. If you want to get better, you have to go back there.*

She wasn't sure that he wanted to get better. There was a high chance that he felt nothing particularly needed improving. Yet, when she saw photos of him that occasionally surfaced on social media, she invariably saw eyes in pain. If not sad, they were defiant. Or drunk. Rarely were they relaxed and happy.

Ignorance and arrogance can so easily be changed by two small changes of heart and mind—willingness to grow and humility. Yet they are so preciously and ridiculously cherished.

And for what? Eyes that betray the depths of existential despair.

THE DREAMING

CHAPTER 28

GADI AND WAMBAD

The Bell and Wambul were running high and fast. They weren't flooding, but it was close. Luna and Maliyan stood in the middle of the bridge crossing Wambul immediately before the Bell joined it for a dance. It would have to be a quickstep—the fastest and jumpiest of the ballroom dances. They leaned over the railing and peered at the loud, brown water. It was somewhat hypnotic.

"A long time ago, in the Dreaming," said Maliyan, "Gadi, the Rainbow Serpent, made the waterways. Water is life. She gave life, but could get angry and destroy life. Gadi travelled through Country to this beautiful valley, Binjang. She needed a resting place to have her babies."

"Who was the father?" asked Luna.

Ignoring Luna's question, Maliyan said, "When the baby snakes were born, Wambad, the wombat, chased them."

"Why?" asked Luna.

"To eat them."

"I thought wombats were vegetarian," said Luna.

"As the babies tried to escape, they formed the rivers and creeks. The first two babies, the biggest and strongest, formed the Wambul and Bell Rivers."

Luna peered at the hurtling water of Wambul and said, "They are like the winning sperm."

"The littler babies formed the smaller rivers and creeks. Some babies weren't fast enough, and Wambad ate them."

Luna was about to point out that his question of the herbivore nature of wombats remained unanswered.

"Gadi was angry and chased Wambad, who tunnelled underground. She followed him, and her body in the tunnels created the caves. Eventually, she caught Wambad and strangled him. He was dead, but that did not bring the babies back. Gadi's tears filled the caves and made underground rivers."

"Not a happy ending," said Luna, attempting to pull Maliyan back from the Dreaming.

CHAPTER 29

LEFT-BRAIN MALFUNCTION

The following day, Maliyan had an appointment with the back doctor in the city. As her back was not improving, he suggested a minor operation. He had a cancellation for the next morning's surgery list and offered the space to her. Her right-brained intuition told her to take it, so she did. The operation went smoothly, and she saw him again on her way home at the end of the week.

"My back is recovering well," said Maliyan, "but I have a question about the general anaesthetic."

The back doctor, a straight-talking, no-nonsense person, said, "Ask me how anaesthetic works."

"We don't know," he replied after Maliyan asked him. "Is it good? Undoubtedly. Do we understand it? Not even close."

❦

MALIYAN STRUGGLED ON THE FIVE-HOUR DRIVE TO Nanima. It was not her back that was the problem. It was the effect of the anaesthetic. A few days after the operation, when the pain-killing drugs had worn off, she noticed that she had to force herself to concentrate on all the left-brained, logical, practical matters in life, such as driving. On the other hand, her right-brained, intuitive, creative side was on fire.

As she drove, her mind drifted into the Dreaming. She remembered a woman she knew in her twenties when her friends started having babies.

The woman had a strange birth experience. It was a caesarean. She had no religious or spiritual inclination but had a life-altering, out-of-body experience when waking from the anaesthetic. She vividly experienced the birth and death of every life she had ever had. Reincarnation was not something she believed in or ever thought about.

She said the whole process was challenging but not disturbing. It was more like watching a movie. She also said the deaths were much more fun and blissful than any of the births. There were an astounding number of lives, and she travelled through them in great detail. Yet, it happened very quickly.

Of course, when she woke up, she tried to tell the nurses. They said it was the anaesthetic. She knew it wasn't.

Her husband believed her, although he didn't know what it all meant. He simply chose to believe her, and that was that.

Every time she went into the baby's room for the first few weeks of his life, she would see the face of a wise, old man instead of seeing a newborn's face. Again, it wasn't disturbing, just perplexing. Gradually, it stopped happening.

Concentrate, Maliyan reprimanded herself as she drove along the country highway, *or I will experience the reincarnation process firsthand!*

CHAPTER 30

WHY?

Relieved to be safely driving into Nanima, Maliyan stopped at Luna Tiks for coffee. She thought it might help her left brain wake up. Luna was in a mood. Even though he hadn't seen her for a week, he took her order without looking and then busied himself with something behind the counter. Maliyan's brain wasn't coming up with a likely explanation for Luna's behaviour, so she called out to him over the empty tables.

"What's the matter? Why aren't you talking to me? I haven't seen you for a whole week."

Luna took one short, annoyed look in her direction and huffed off into the back room. When he was angry, he wasn't poisonous. He was by no means a pushover—independent people aren't—but he didn't have intent to harm. Besides, almost everything he did seemed to have an element of humour in it. He had such a strong, natural leaning towards seeing the funny side of life that it tended to stick with him, whether he wanted it or not.

As Maliyan walked out, she realised that he must have missed her.

I'll tell him where I have been tomorrow when he has calmed down, she thought.

Even with only half of her brain working, she knew the limits of his sense of humour. And his feelings.

KEEN TO SET THINGS RIGHT, MALIYAN HEADED FOR Luna Tiks on her walk the following morning. However, her happy, hopeful moment of setting things right turned into the opposite when she saw Luna walking into the cafe, arm in arm, with a woman. Maliyan recognised her— a bright, fiery young thing, recently appointed head of the new Cultural Centre. When she read about the appointment, she thought it was an excellent choice for the town.

Suddenly, nothing made sense. Maliyan wondered if it was her muddled brain getting things more muddled. She wondered if her gut reaction was wrong. After all, Luna was generally an affectionate person. Even if her gut reaction was right, what was she upset about? Maybe Luna hadn't missed her at all. Perhaps it was only she who had missed him.

As neither her left nor her right brain was helping her feel less confused, she decided to bypass Luna Tiks, head for the Wambul, and watch the racing water until it quietened her racing heart.

BREATH-BASED

CHAPTER 31

SOMETHING THERE

As Maliyan walked into Luna Tiks, the woman she had seen with Luna was walking out.

"That's the person I was telling you about," said Luna. "The one who is always banging on about the bones—the Repatriation Program—and now she's head of the new Cultural Centre."

Detecting a note of pride in Luna, Maliyan looked deeply into his eyes.

"Where have you been?" he asked, diverting attention from himself. "I haven't seen you for a few weeks."

"I had a week in the city after a back operation that I didn't know I was going to have."

"And why are children running around your front yard?" asked Luna. "Do you have children that I don't know about? Did you bring them back with you from the city?"

Maliyan laughed and said, "Of course not. I've rented my house to them."

"Where are you living?"

"Euroka's."

"Are you living with him?"

"Of course not," repeated Maliyan. "He has gone to Uluru."

She changed her tone and added, "He said he is going to die there."

Luna didn't know how to respond to that.

"He'll be back," he said, picking up some plates and cups.

"I'm not so sure," said Maliyan. "He gave away all his furniture and donated his artworks to the Cultural Centre."

Luna put the plates down again.

"He gave me his hut," said Maliyan in an understated manner. "He said I don't have to live there and am free to do anything I want with it."

"Then sell it," said Luna. "Don't live there. It's freezing. Euroka is much tougher than you. And the river floods."

"Yes, he is," said Maliyan, "but I've blocked up most of the holes and got my fire-making system running smoothly. The flood waters only occasionally get that high."

Luna raised his hands in a *why* gesture.

"There is something there," said Maliyan.

"I'm sure there is something there," said Luna, who looked like it would be wisest to leave *the something* to itself.

As Maliyan left, she handed Luna a piece of paper and said, "Can you please do this and tell me what happens?"

CHAPTER 32

UP AND DRESSED

L ate winter wasn't the best time to move into
Euroka's hut. Then again, Maliyan wasn't sure if
there was an ideal time to move into a primitive
hut haunted by spirits. The fire hadn't had a chance to
make a dent in the morning chill, and she watched her
foggy breath as she practised her new breathing exercises.

Among the few items Euroka left behind in a box was
an old book called *Breath-Based Yogic Practice*. Maliyan's
eyes fell on a chapter called *Shambhavi Mahamudra*, which
outlined a 21-minute exercise as follows:

1. Start with slow alternate-nostril breathing for 6 or 7 minutes. It helps to balance the mind.
2. Then, do 21 long repetitions of Om (Aum). Make sure you pass through the three stages of ah-uu-mm, as each stage activates different energy centres. *Ah* is for creation, *uu* is for manifestation, and *mm* is for destruction. Creation needs all three.
3. Next, do the quick, shallow nose-breathing exercise, Viparita Swasa, for 3 to 4 minutes.
4. Move on to breath retention on the inhale and then on the exhale, while muscularly and energetically engaging the bandhas—the pelvic floor, lower abdomen, and throat.
5. Lastly, sit quietly in meditation for 5 minutes.

It carried a warning not to practise the exercise unless one had been given appropriate instruction and had been initiated into it by a suitable teacher.

As Maliyan had neither appropriate instruction nor suitable teacher, she decided to initiate herself into it. She hoped that the combined spirits of Euroka's hut and the Bell River would assist with her venture.

1. The alternate nostril breathing was easy and relaxing. Maliyan felt that, as the book stated, most people would find it balancing.
2. The 21 repetitions of Aum were more work, but she assumed they were meant to be as the exercise touched the whole spectrum of creation—no little feat.
3. The rapid, shallow nose breathing was beyond her. *This damn thing,* she would mutter every time she got to it. She felt that all she was managing to do was hyperventilate. However, for all her complaining, she noticed that it had the strange effect of bringing a great deal of energy (which felt like fire) into her body, particularly her lower chakras.
4. She found the breath retention and bandha locks relatively straightforward and enjoyable. It was as if all the fire that had accumulated in her body from the previous exercise was being put to good use. What *the good use* was, she didn't know.

Deciding to keep reading the book, she saw a note after the breathing instructions.

Note to Women:
You may find that this combination of exercises directly affects the activation of sexual energy in your body. We recommend using it in an appropriate energetic way.

She was interested in the note because she had already mentally and physically noted the effect herself.

Appropriate energetic way? thought Maliyan. *What is that when it's up and dressed?* (a saying her country relatives sometimes used)

I wonder what it tells men to do? her thoughts continued.

She turned the page, but it was torn out. And that is how she came to copy the breathing exercise and give it to Luna without an explanation.

❧

A FEW DAYS LATER, IN LUNA TIKS:

"I've been too busy to do your breathing exercises," said Luna off-handedly.

"That's okay," said Maliyan. "You don't have to do them. Only if you want to."

Luna looked like that wouldn't be any time soon.

"Are you dating that woman who is the head of the Cultural Centre?" asked Maliyan, deciding that honesty saves a lot of time and confusion.

"Nah, I'm not partner-able," said Luna. "No one could stand me."

Maliyan opened her mouth to reply, but Luna continued, "And I couldn't stand anyone."

If you don't have time to do my breathing exercises, which would do you a world of good, thought Maliyan, *and you don't want to make an effort to include anyone in your personal life, then I'll leave you to your own miserable self.*

As Maliyan pulled on her coat to leave, Luna said, slightly apologetically, "I'll get back to you."

Maliyan didn't bother answering.

BODY-BASED

CHAPTER 33

BE A MAN

"**S**he told me to be a man about it," said the guy sitting near Maliyan in the city cafe.

As she was early for her appointment, Maliyan was waiting in the cafe next door to the Chiropractic Centre. Sensing an interesting conversation, her eyes focused on the nearby man—trendy, attractive, middle-aged, gym-toned.

"You can be a man about things even if you are gay," said a familiar voice. "She meant to be honest."

The voice belonged to Gary. Maliyan felt that she probably should move or, at least, let him know she was there, but she didn't.

"I *was* honest with her," objected the man. "I told her I am gay. What more does she want from me?"

"What else did Christina say?" asked Gary.

"If you really want to know," said the man, "she said, 'Don't fucking give me that. This is not about being gay. I don't fucking care if you are gay or not. You think that if you say those two magic words, it makes everything excusable. It's not fucking excusable. Tell the goddam truth. Say that you don't want to be with me, or say that you want to be with someone else, or say that you don't want a relationship anymore, or say that you are bored, or say that you are tired, or say any fucking thing except that you are gay, which supposedly entitles you to be as vague, irresponsible, and hurtful as you want. Do you think other people can get away with that? No, every other grown-up has to work out their relationships. They don't get to say they are gay and prance off whenever they please. Everyone else has to talk about things, think about the other person, respect their commitments, and try to get what they want in life with the least amount of damage to other people's feelings. Grow up, Sebastian! Be a man about it!"

"She's angry," said Gary. "You can't blame her. She's hurt. There's some truth in what she says. I don't get to prance off whenever I want. I have to go through the torturous process of talking about things. What man wants to talk things through?"

Maliyan laughed. Gary heard her voice and turned towards her.

"Oh, I'm so sorry," said Maliyan, "I didn't mean to eavesdrop [which was a total lie]."

"This is my brother," said Gary.

Sebastian held out his hand and said, "Yeah, I'm gay."

All three laughed, and Sebastian said he had to go and sort out his life.

"At least he has a sense of humour," said Maliyan when it was only Gary and her.

Gary pulled his chair closer to Maliyan and said, "He does, but I don't know how much humour will help him with Christina."

CHAPTER 34

OWN IT

"Sex is difficult for people to talk about," said Gary. "Believe me, I know. If we talked about it properly, it would probably eliminate most of the ridiculous things said about it."

Maliyan nodded and said, "Simple honesty about our physical bodies, how they function, and what they need to be balanced and healthy gets rid of so many unnecessary problems."

"It's like money," said Gary. "People also find that a prickly conversation. They whinge and hassle each other but have trouble discussing it directly."

After hesitating, Gary continued, "You remind me of my longtime friend. She is very spiritual. Not like me. That's probably why we aren't together. We fight."

I thought you wouldn't be together because you are married to someone else, thought Maliyan.

Her second thought was surprise at his claim that he was not spiritual, since she saw that as a significant component of his energy field.

"It's strange that you say you are not spiritual," said Maliyan.

"No, I'm not," said Gary. "I always fought with her about it. I thought she was over the top. She thought I was way too low. Even now, we can only see each other for short catch-ups, or the conversation quickly deteriorates. I'm one end of the spectrum. She's the other."

"Maybe you push that part of yourself onto another person," said Maliyan, "because you don't feel comfortable with it. People do that all the time. They don't know what to do with some aspect of themselves, so they project it onto another person and then end up fighting with that person. They are fighting with themselves."

Gary's trust in Maliyan touched her. She recalled a conversation in Luna Tiks some months ago when the dancing hunter unexpectedly told her about his love of the outback and how it was the only place he felt at ease. His vulnerability in the situation caused him to go up significantly in her estimation.

I have little time for people who don't have the capacity for vulnerability and honesty, thought Maliyan. *You never get anywhere with them.*

LIVING IN A RIVER

CHAPTER 35

MRS KNUCKLE AND
THE SPINSTERS

The closest neighbour to Euroka's hut was Mrs Knuckle. Although Maliyan hadn't seen her for decades, she knew who she was because her great aunts often spoke about her when Maliyan was a child. The great aunts were spinsters.

What a dreadful word to describe single women, thought Maliyan, *but, at the time, that's what unmarried women were called when they were considered too old to be in the market anymore. Maybe I'm a spinster.*

Mrs Knuckle, who wasn't a spinster, took Maliyan's great aunts under her wing. She always seemed a mystery to Maliyan, not least because she was a tea-leaf reader. Her great aunts were forever relaying Mrs Knuckle's highly valued readings. As Maliyan recalled, most readings had "a tall, dark, handsome man" in them. Lacking male company, the great aunts never tired of their ponderings about the tall, dark, handsome strangers.

After seeing Mrs Knuckle in her garden, Maliyan decided to introduce herself. She had to repeat herself numerous times because Mrs Knuckle, who would have been well into her nineties, didn't hear very well. When she offered Maliyan a cup of tea (and presumably a free tea-leaf reading), she couldn't resist.

They weaved in and out of furniture, boxes, and knick-knacks to get to the reading room, which was the place where all good speculations are born—the kitchen. The table was covered with a clean, white cloth with tiny embroidered flowers. Maliyan fingered the delicate embroidery admiringly as she drank her tea.

Nothing like carefully brewed tea in fine china on a hand-sewn tablecloth, she thought as she passed her empty cup to Mrs Knuckle.

"Interesting," said Mrs Knuckle. "Very interesting."

"What is it?" asked Maliyan. "Is it a tall, dark, handsome man?"

Mrs Knuckle looked up from the cup and said, "No. Do you want a tall, dark, handsome man? I suggest the dating sites."

That shut Maliyan up. Placing the cup in the sink full of washing-up water, Mrs Knuckle pulled her hand out and watched the water drip off it.

"The flood will be here soon," said Mrs Knuckle.

"Is that what you saw in my cup?" asked Maliyan.

"No," said Mrs Knuckle. "I can feel it in my waters. And I heard it on the radio this morning."

Mrs Knuckle was proving to be as much of an enigma as when Maliyan was a child.

"I move to my sister's house before the water gets here," said Mrs Knuckle.

"When will it be here?" asked Maliyan anxiously.

Shuffling outside, Mrs Knuckle looked up at the trees and slowly bent down to pick up some dirt.

"Soon," she said.

Without saying goodbye, she went back inside and started packing her things to leave.

CHAPTER 36

NANIMARIANS

Achala, the new head of the Cultural Centre, and a man who was some sort of river management employee were discussing the coming flood in Luna Tiks.

"No floods, no flood plains," said Achala. "That's what the elders say. The floodplains are part of the river. It's not that the river rudely encroaches on our territory. The floodplains are more river than land. We can't take the benefit and complain about the price."

If the floodplains are more river than land, thought Maliyan, *then I am living in a river.*

"We must find a better way of working with the process, not against it," said the man. "All the intervention has only made matters worse. Flooding can be disastrous for humans, but the floodplains are incredible and important ecosystems."

"Hello, darling," said Luna, hugging Maliyan and pulling her eyes and ears away from the flood conversation.

Maliyan started telling Luna all about Mrs Knuckle,

but was interrupted by a couple with mild intellectual disability who ran up to him and demanded attention. The woman had returned to Nanima this morning from a week's hospital stay in Thubbo.

"You'll be glad to have each other back in the same bed," said Luna.

Many people would consider the intimate relationship of a disabled couple uncomfortable. Not Luna. It seemed to Maliyan that those who fit in most naturally at Luna Tiks all had something slightly unusual about them. It could be anything. Something that wasn't quite straight-down-the-line conventional.

Only one type of person didn't fit in at Luna Tiks— class-conscious, conservative folk. Whenever one of them inadvertently wandered in, Luna got a certain look of distaste on his face. They didn't tend to return, so it must have been mutual.

Generally, however, Luna Tiks was a place to belong. Luna called his people *Nanimarians.* Well-functioning cafes make a significant contribution to their communities' mental health.

On the other side of Maliyan's table was a family grouping of two men and several young children. When they left, Maliyan quietly asked Luna if it was a couple and their kids.

"Nope, stranger than that," said Luna. "It's the ex-husband and current husband. They do the swap-over of children because the wife is busy at work. As they enjoy each other's company, they meet here for a meal. And the bags, news, and kids get swapped over for the week."

"Unless you have somewhere else to stay," said Luna, "you'd better stay here with us until the flood has gone."

Iggy sat up and looked like company was an excellent idea.

"Alright," said Maliyan. "Thanks."

"Also," said Luna, "I decided to take your advice about Achala. I'm going to ask her out."

That wasn't my advice, thought Maliyan.

"Alright," she said for the second time.

Iggy put his head back on the floor and looked like it would be wisest to abstain from having an opinion about the matter.

THE WRONG WAY

CHAPTER 37

HAVE TO—WANT TO

S pring had plenty of spring in its step as it leapt into its longed-for day. Maliyan looked through the front window of Luna Tiks, watching Kat across the road.

Kat, her husband, and their ten-year-old son were packing up the dance school. The husband's work project in Thubbo had unexpectedly come to a halt, and they were heading back to the city.

He patted Kat on the bum as she passed him, hands full. They had been married for a long time, not out of duty—out of desire. Not just physical desire (although there was still plenty of that), but desire to keep creating the life they were making together. They were both the sort of people who could easily re-partner if ever there was a need. That is a good position to be in. And stay in.

Ding. Maliyan's phone had a new message.

REX

Thanks. Sorry to hear the dance school is closing.

Rex was replying to the birthday wish she had sent him this morning.

MALIYAN

> Not to worry. Maybe something else will turn up.

Birthdays are a day for being grateful that someone exists, thought Maliyan. *We shouldn't take it for granted. What if they died tomorrow? They could. Anyone could. We should say what we want without fear of it being taken the wrong way.*

MALIYAN

> You were the best thing that happened to my dancing.

Maliyan felt two hands on her shoulders.

"Who are you talking to?" asked Luna, peering at her phone.

"No one," said Maliyan.

Luna pulled a face at her.

"How's Achala going?" asked Maliyan brightly.

"Great," said Luna. "She's going great!"

CHAPTER 38

ENTANGLED

Indeed, Achala was going great. Maliyan saw her in the park on the way home. She was lying on the grass, enjoying the first days of warmer weather and the not-so-soggy soil.

She had her body entwined around a man who was also enjoying the weather... and her.

"I DON'T MEAN TO BE THE BEARER OF BAD NEWS," SAID Maliyan that afternoon in Luna Tiks, "but I saw your new love interest in the park, and she appears to have more interests than you."

"Yeah, that's her husband," said Luna.

"She's married?" asked Maliyan. "Then why did you say you were dating her?"

"Because you were staying in my house during the flood," said Luna, "and I didn't want you to take it the wrong way."

"That's insulting," said Maliyan.

She went back out into the sunshine, past the empty dance studio that seemed to have already reverted to its semi-derelict state, and back to the river.

My God, she thought as she watched the bouncing water, *with the number of times people have to forgive each other for big and little, real and imagined transgressions, it's a wonder that anyone's relationships ever survive!*

GRAVE CONCERN

CHAPTER 39

ANCESTOR RESPECTER

I t took nine months, but finally, Maliyan drove the twenty minutes out of Nanima to the tiny town that was the place of her family's history and burial. The original farm of her grandfather was further out, deeper into bush. Over the years, the property expanded with land acquisition closer to town. Grandfather's house was left to the elements from which it came.

Nowadays, it was a quicker drive from Nanima to the tiny town because the dirt road had been sealed. Although it was a more comfortable ride, Maliyan could not help feeling a tinge of concern that the place of her roots, which had thankfully always seemed so far removed from the city and the world, was losing its invisibility. So much of its beauty and power came from its isolation and inaccessibility. The dust and bumps of the dirt road had kept all but locals and family away. Too hot, cold, shopless, activityless, and uncivilised for most, the town retained a marvellous sense of having its own reality.

Anyway, out there, you had to concentrate on other things—how to keep warm in homes that only had one wood stove in the kitchen, how to cool down with relent-less heat beating on uninsulated tin roofs, how to keep the flys away when picking peaches in the orchard, how to stop the incessant itch of peach fluff in the packing shed with talcum powder, and how to outsmart the vicious and mad attacks of the rooster.

Her first stop was the graveyard. The condition of the little bush cemetery varied depending on who the care-taker was. Sometimes, the locals cared for it. Sometimes, the council. Council was hit and miss. So were the locals. Some were dedicated ancestor respecters, and the ceme-tery was mowed religiously. Some left the relatives to fend for themselves, in which case, you would be strategically jumping through snake-infested, long grass. Cemeteries are ideal for snakes.

Maliyan wandered among the graves and tried to recall the lineage so often told to her by her aunt up the hill. It seemed a little irrelevant at the time, but as we get older, so does our realisation of the DNA we carry in our bodies, hearts, and minds. Not knowing it does not negate it. We are an accumulation of many people, even more so when unaware of it. Once aware, we can choose what to carry and what to relegate to history.

As much as she tried to sort the lineage out, it remained muddled. There were too many Marys, Anns, Michaels and Johns on her relatives' gravestones to distin-guish their correct placing.

She wiped the dust off the black marble stone of her parents' grave and sat on it. Looking at the newish grave next to her parents, she smiled as she recalled her uncle-up-the-hill's annoyance that a non-relative had chosen the spot.

Apparently, he said, "I don't like him. If I knew he was going to put himself there, I would have stopped it."

He didn't like most people. When he liked you, he loved you.

The dead were never far away from Maliyan. However, here in the cemetery, in this special place of her bloodline, it was pumping with energetic life. The line between the worlds was blurring.

The spring morning had a bit of biting wind. The grave was in a relatively sheltered spot, so Maliyan hugged the sun-warmed marble slab closer. Being lulled deeper into the spirits of the deceased and the Spirit of the land, she lay back on it. It seemed like it would be such a tiny step to cross the blurry division of worlds. Such a thin line.

The sound of a distant car brought her back. She thought that if someone saw her lying motionless on her parents' grave, they might have grave concerns for her mental health.

In the country, there are unseen eyes and ears everywhere. They may not be many in number, but they are highly perceptive. That's what happens when you live in a quiet environment. You notice everything.

Further, it gets passed on fast—the notorious *bush telegraph*.

CHAPTER 40

DOWN THE HILL

A figure appeared at the top of the hill. The farm of Maliyan's uncle backed onto the cemetery. He was slowly making his way down the paddock, past the sheep, to the cemetery fence. She had seen him occasionally at family gatherings but had not visited the farm in many years.

"Ahh, you're back," he called out.

Maliyan gave him her arm as they climbed up the hill to the homestead. He only reluctantly accepted it.

"I'll make you a cup of tea," he said once he caught his breath in the stove-warmed kitchen. It was a privilege to be made a cup of tea by him. "My tea maker is down the hill," he said, pointing to the cemetery. He missed her stingingly. "I'll be there too before long."

"Not yet," said Maliyan, urging him to resist the pull down the hill.

"When then?" he asked.

Her uncle had somewhat softened to the things he neither understood nor wanted in Maliyan. Besides, when you have watched someone from childhood, you know them. You know what they came with, even if you don't like it. Young children don't pretend to be something they are not. They don't even know how to. They only know what they are.

Given the invitation, Maliyan stared into her uncle's eyes and energy field. He laughed from nervousness but let her continue.

His body has some serious physical problems, thought Maliyan. *And his pain level is high.*

She wanted to cry when she felt his pain, but how insulting to cry because we don't like to see the suffering that someone else has to live with every day. Some of his problems were self-created. Some were age-related. It didn't matter where they came from. Not now.

"You're a tough bugger," said Maliyan, smiling.

Her uncle took that as a great compliment and turned up one corner of his lined mouth. Bushmen are understated in just about every way—their words, their affection, their need for things. They don't need much of anything. They're understated except when it comes to hard work and duty. His resilience and determination to get out into the paddocks every day would, to an extent, keep at bay the bottom of the hill. Being outside, in the elements, added substantial weight to his life force.

"Not yet," repeated Maliyan. "It's not time yet. Keep going."

Sometimes, it is kindest to help senior folk pass on as peacefully and well as possible rather than pushing them to stay. In this situation, although she didn't want him to suffer, she felt that, due to his ability to mentally and physically tough it out, he could benefit from a soul perspective. The last few years of some people's lives earn them more advancement on the spiritual path than several life-times put together.

After an hour, Maliyan could see that he was tired, so she said she would head back down the paddock, through the cemetery, to her car.

Her uncle looked at her with weepy old-man eyes, both brave and scared, and said, "You came home."

LIFE HAPPENS

CHAPTER 41

BRIDGE IS DOWN

S ometimes on her morning walk, Maliyan joined the small, loyal gathering in the Catholic church for weekday Mass. The priest, a born and bred country lad, usually gave a short talk. Knowing that Maliyan had been absent from Nanima for decades, he thought about things that happened during her absence and weaved them into his story whenever he saw her sitting in the pews.

Referring to the recent death of the monarch, the priest said with rural humour, "I'm just about Elizabeth Windsor'd out. And we still have a coronation to come!"

He continued, more solemnly, "As we now all know, the code used to communicate the Queen's death to the prime minister and other important personnel was, 'London Bridge is down.' This reminded me of the fatal falling of our bridge thirty years ago, which many of you will remember.

At the time, I was a young priest in a nearby town. When I visited my older counterpart here, he told me an interesting story. He said,

'This morning, I walked down to the fallen bridge to see if I could assist in any way. Halfway there, I came to Mr Parkins. You know what a cata-strophising complainer he is. True to style, he went on a long, depressing tirade about the death of our town now that the bridge had collapsed.

When I was almost at the bridge, I came across young Jimmy Jenkins with his unruly hair, bare feet, and bright clothes.

He had made a little stand and was selling T-shirts that said, *Welcome to the town where the bridge fell down!*"'

Father concluded the talk with, "Life happens. Death happens. It all depends on how we respond to it."

CHAPTER 42

BEWITCHED

After morning Mass, the Rosary began. Normally, Maliyan didn't stay for it, but today she felt like listening to its chant-like, lulling rhythm. It essentially consists of one Our Father and ten Hail Marys, repeated ten times. Father began the prayer.

> Our Father,
> who art in heaven,
> hallowed be thy name;
> thy kingdom come;
> thy will be done on Earth as it is in heaven.

The little group responded with the rest of the Our Father.

Give us this day our daily bread;
and forgive us our trespasses
as we forgive those who trespass against us;
and lead us not into temptation,
but deliver us from evil.
Amen

Father then started on the ten Hail Marys.

Hail Mary, full of grace.
The Lord is with thee.
Blessed art thou among women,
and blessed is the fruit of thy womb,
Jesus.

The group responded.

Holy Mary, Mother of God,
pray for us sinners,
now and at the hour of our death.
Amen

After the tenth Hail Mary, instead of continuing the lead himself, the priest passed it on to the congregation member sitting on his right. Maliyan counted the people to Father's right. She was the fifth.

Uh oh, she thought. *Everyone is taking a turn at leading. That means I will have to lead.*

Any Catholic knows these prayers by heart, backwards and forwards. However, the strange thing is that under pressure to perform, we often can't. Words long since relegated to our deep memory cells seem to muddle and vanish into thin air.

She recalled that in the thirteenth century, a spoken test was introduced in place of the fire test for suspected witches. The theologians, priests, and lawyers of the time believed it to be a more civilised test than determining whether the suspect would burn in fire. All the accused had to do was to say the prayer that everyone knew from childhood—the Our Father—faultlessly in the courtroom. Not surprisingly, the suspects failed almost as much as they did in the fire test.

The person next to Maliyan finished their recitation of the last Hail Mary.

When all seemed doomed, the hand of the Divine intervened, and Father said, "I have to do an early funeral today. I'm so sorry, but we need to cut the Rosary short."

Maliyan was saved from the bewitching flames!

PLAYING AROUND

CHAPTER 43

DIDGERIDOO

Next to the box with Euroka's book, *Breath-Based Yogic Practice*, were several didgeridoos. Maliyan had played with the idea of playing them ever since she moved in a few months ago. The didgeridoo's voice is the voice of the tree from which it is made. Every didgeridoo is unique. It blends its spirit with the player to create a distinctive combination of energy.

Maliyan fingered the didgeridoos carefully. She could easily tell which one was Euroka's. It *felt* like Euroka and was the largest and most heavily decorated. The medium-sized one felt like it already had a person, but Maliyan didn't know them. The smallest one felt person-less, so she started using it. She knew that some Aboriginals do not like non-Aboriginals playing them. Also, some think they are not for women at all—Aboriginal or not.

The didgeridoo is played by vibrating the lips to produce a continuous drone. When played properly, a breathing technique called circular breathing is used. Maliyan thought that there was probably a yogic equivalent to circular breathing. However, her aspiration was only to play around, not to play proficiently. So, she settled for making low guttural sounds and doing her twenty-one slow repetitions of Om/Aum for Shambhavi Mahamudra through the didgeridoo. That worked quite well. So well that she started doing it next to the river for added effect. No one was close enough to hear—except the spirits of the river.

Like practising Shambhavi Mahamudra, playing the didgeridoo had an earthy, physical, stabilising effect on the body. First Nations people needed strong lower chakras for survival and health in harsh terrains.

Maliyan rested the end of the didgeridoo on the edge of the bank. Occasionally, she rested it in the river. The primal sound reverberated through the water, amplifying its effect. It gurgled through her body, into the Bell, towards the Wambul.

She found a note in Euroka's box that read, *You don't make the sound. The sound makes you.* Not sure whether the note was referring to the didgeridoo, she nevertheless mentally repeated the words as she played.

The sound makes you.
The sound makes you.
The sound makes you.

"The sound makes you," Maliyan said to the Bell. "The sound makes me. The sound of creation throws its fire into all I want to make in my life."

Other than the Bell, there was someone else listening to Maliyan's music and musings. A shadow sat on the slope a little further down the river.

It was Mrs Knuckle.

CHAPTER 44

BUSH TELEGRAPH

The following day, Luna had a new customer. He recognised the old lady from around town and recalled what Maliyan had told him about her. It was Mrs Knuckle.

"To what do we owe the pleasure of your company, young lady?" said Luna in his most charming manner.

"Don't belittle me with your condescending flattery," Mrs Knuckle said.

Luna was taken aback but quickly recovered. He had a quick mind. It was one of his assets. He also knew when he was wrong. Even more important.

"How can I help you?" he said apologetically.

"I believe you are friends with my neighbour, Maliyan," said Mrs Knuckle.

"Yes, why?" asked Luna.

"There's something wrong with her," continued Mrs Knuckle.

"Why?" asked Luna again.

"I don't know why," said Mrs Knuckle. "I'm not a mind reader!"

Luna thought he detected a gleam in her eye.

"She sits in the river below my house and makes all sorts of weird noises," said Mrs Knuckle.

"Really?" said Luna with growing concern. "What sort of weird noises?"

He didn't put it past her to be doing exactly that. It worried him. That was another of Luna's strong points. He cared. He didn't care about everyone. He wasn't evolved enough for that. But he cared deeply about certain bits of life. Nothing wonderful can ever grow in us if we do not give our heart to life or, at least, to specific bits of life that we deem appropriate and desirable.

"God only knows," said Mrs Knuckle. "Sometimes, I think she's drowning because of all the gurgling sounds she makes."

God might know what she's doing, thought Luna, *but no one else does. She needs to get out of that place. There are too many spirits down there. And she's turning into one of them.*

Without buying anything and without saying goodbye, Mrs Knuckle left the cafe. Once outside, she relaxed, smiled wryly, and turned her mind to the long (at her age) journey home.

༄

A FEW DAYS AGO, ONE OF LUNA'S REGULAR CUSTOMERS came in and said after ordering, "You're buddies with that woman down at Euroka's, aren't you?"

"Yes, why?" asked Luna.

"My Dad lives out of town," said the man, "and he saw someone lying on one of the gravestones. He told the publican, who told some of the local farmers. One of the farmers said, 'Yeah, yeah. That would be my niece. She visited the other day. Don't mind 'er. She's like that.'"

Luna made a joke, and the two men moved on to something else. Luna's thoughts, however, did not move on so quickly.

THE SOUND MAKES YOU

CHAPTER 45

BREAK AND REMAKE

"Just letting you know that my wife and I will be away travelling for the next few months," messaged Gary, the chiropractor.

"Thanks," replied Maliyan. "How are things?"

"Looking forward to a long break," replied Gary. "I thought you'd be glad to hear that my brother and his wife have made progress with their situation."

"That's great," said Maliyan.

"As you know from overhearing Sebastian's conversation, Christina was mad as a cut snake," said Gary. "However, after a while, she got really sad, sort of depressed. We were worried about her. Sebastian said that he could handle her anger but not her sadness. He would hear her muffled cries in the bedroom, and he said it broke his heart."

"Love" breaks everyone's heart, thought Maliyan. *If we are fortunate, it then remakes it.*

Gary continued, "Christina recently said to Sebastian, 'I feel it would be a good idea for us to continue living under the same roof for the coming year. It'll be family life as usual, except that we'll have our own bedrooms. We can make something up so the kids don't worry. You are free to go out wherever you want, with whoever you want, and no questions will be asked. At the end of the year, we can reassess our relationship and decide what we both want to do.' Frankly, I was shocked by the calm maturity of the whole thing."

"That may save their marriage," said Maliyan, "and if not, they will both be the better for it and move on without undue stress."

CHAPTER 46

COMMUNICATION NETWORK

A knock at the hut door brought Maliyan out of her musings about Christina and Sebastian.

"Euroka!" said Maliyan, touching his arm.

Euroka laughed and said, "Are you checking to see what sort of spirit I am?"

"Did you make it to Uluru?" asked Maliyan.

"Yes," said Euroka.

Sensing her next question, he added, "Yes, I did die—a death of sorts."

He strode into the clearing between his hut and the Bell, picked up two sticks from the ground, and banged them together several times. The sound reverberated around the old gums. It's what Aboriginal people do to let their ancestors know they would like to respectfully enter the space.

"Take your time. No rush to find somewhere else," said Euroka.

"How will I tell you when I find somewhere to move to?" Maliyan called to Euroka as he headed into the bush.

"No need," said Euroka. "I'll know."

His bush telegraph doesn't rely on other people, thought Maliyan. *It's a different sort of communication network—much faster and much more reliable.*

CHAPTER 47

RETURN

L una couldn't sleep. He got up when it was still dark and walked down to the Bell. He kept walking and eventually got to Euroka's hut. Seeing Maliyan's light on, he quietly knocked on the door.

"Is everything alright?" asked Maliyan.

"I was walking past and saw you were already awake," said Luna with uncharacteristic seriousness.

Maliyan waited for him to continue.

He looked at the ground, the river, and then Maliyan. Nothing made it easier, so he just said what he came to say.

"I think you should move back into my house."

Staring at him intently, Maliyan said, "Oh, I know what has happened."

"You do?" said Luna.

"Yes," said Maliyan. "The bush telegraph has been at work."

Luna shuffled uncomfortably.

"Someone told you that Euroka is back," said Maliyan.

"Yes," said Luna, trying not to look surprised that Euroka had returned.

Unknown to Maliyan, Euroka had made sure that no one saw him.

"You caught me out," said Luna. "You know how it is with the bush telegraph. Can't beat it for gossip."

After quickly packing a few things, Maliyan ran her hand down the didgeridoo and thought, *I better leave this here. If we want to play around with the spirits without bodies, we must be very sure where home is. Otherwise, we can drift so far away that it can be hard to return.*

Meandering along the river's edge, back to Luna Tiks, they both watched the early light skimming here and there over the gentle water. A deep sense of stability and happiness emanated from the Bell as it rang out its mantra.

The sound makes you.
The sound makes you.
The sound makes you.

The End

SUMMARY OF NANIMA SERIES

A contemplative journey of spiritual evolution, soulful relationships, and the quiet healing power of nature.

Spanning four deeply personal and spiritually rich books—Nanima, Geboor, Sonder, and The Flat—this series follows Maliyan, an insightful and grounded seeker whose path unfolds across the quiet towns and wild landscapes of rural Australia.

Through shifting relationships, ancestral stirrings, and encounters with both seen and unseen guides, Maliyan's life becomes a mirror for our own inner transformation. Alongside her are Luna—intuitive, witty, and playfully avoidant as he learns to love truly—and Bell-Bell, whose brilliance and volatility reflect the challenges of change and the yearning for wholeness.

The *Nanima Series* offers not just a story, but a spiritual companion. It invites you to walk the path of growth gently, to listen deeply to the land and your own spirit, and to remember that evolution is both quiet and profound.

ABOUT THE AUTHOR

Donna Goddard is a spiritual author whose work blends clarity, devotion, and metaphysical insight. With more than twenty published books across spiritual nonfiction, fiction, poetry, and children's literature, she writes to uplift consciousness and offer healing through words.

In Wellington, Australia, the rural town on which Nanima is based.

Donna's Facebook author page has over 400,000 followers worldwide, and her YouTube channel has received 4 million views. Her books are read by spiritual seekers globally and are known for their honesty, poetic style, and transformative energy.

Her writing is an offering—to help others awaken their own inner spirit, trust its guidance, and create a life of depth, beauty, and quiet joy.

All links at https://linktr.ee/donnagoddard

RATINGS AND REVIEWS

Donna would be grateful for any ratings or reviews.

ALSO BY DONNA GODDARD

Fiction
Waldmeer Series: A Spiritual Fiction Series
Nanima Series: Spiritual Fiction
Enanika Series: Visionary Fiction
Riverland Series (children's fiction 6 to 9 years)
Foxie (children's fiction 7 to 12 years)

Nonfiction
Love and Devotion Series
Sweet Spirit Series
Consciousness Series
Meditation Series
Poetry Series
Love's Longing
Dance: A Spiritual Affair
Writing: A Spiritual Voice

www.ingramcontent.com/pod-product-compliance
Lightning Source LLC
Chambersburg PA
CBHW020522120726
47904CB00003B/928